yip!
yarp!
yip!

yarp!
yarp!

yarp!
yarp!
yarp!

Mister
Got To Go
and Arnie

Story by Lois Simmie

Illustrations by Cynthia Nugent

RAINCOAST BOOKS

Vancouver

In an old hotel covered with vines, there lived

a large grey cat called Got To Go. Across the street from the hotel was the ocean—well, some of it anyway—and a beach where people liked to swim in the summer and walk on the promenade all year round. People especially liked the Sylvia Hotel because of the beach.

In the long, wet winters, Got To Go sat at a window and watched the foolish people walking their foolish dogs in the rain.

Got To Go hated the rain, and the dogs didn't much care for it either, except for the silly ones that would chase a stick over and

over and over. Every time their person threw the stick, they'd tear off after it as if it was something wonderful. Like a nice piece of fish, or one of Miss Pritchett's tuna sandwiches. Got To Go sensibly stayed inside where it was nice and warm, sleeping on the windowsills and riding up and down in the service elevator.

Every so often Mister Foster, the hotel manager, would look at him and say "My word, is that cat still here? As soon as it stops raining, that cat's got to go." But nobody paid any attention. Least of all Got To Go, who had been there seven years.

Got To Go liked summer best.

Then the sun shone and children played in the water at the edge of the ocean, which sparkled under the sun with its frill of happy children. Lots of people walked and ran on the promenade, or zoomed along with little round things on the bottom of their shoes. And peculiar things with long tails swooped and fluttered in the air, while the popcorn man called out "Hot buttered popcorn!

Come and get your popcorn!"

Then Got To Go liked to sit on the windowsill outside and feel the sun on his thick grey fur.

He stayed away from the beach because in summer there were even more dogs chasing sticks

and barking their fool heads off. He went for leisurely strolls

around the hotel or climbed the big tree to see what he could

see. And life was good at the Sylvia Hotel. It

was very good. Until one day.

That day, he heard something that sounded like a dog

bark inside the hotel. In Mister Foster's office.

Got To Go, on his lobby windowsill, kept looking out the

window, but one ear pointed toward Mister Foster's office.

Then Mister Foster came out carrying a creature too little

to be a dog. But when it saw Got To Go it barked.

It was a dog.

A very small dog.

A very small, very noisy dog.

"Oh," said Miss Pritchett the desk clerk, "isn't he darling?"

"Nice little pooch," said Old Harry the bellhop, patting its little head with hair sticking up everywhere and hanging down over its beady little eyes.

Mister Foster carried it over to the windowsill. "Got To Go, this is Arnie," he said.

Arnie barked and barked.

Yip
Yip

Yarp!
Yarp!

Got To Go jumped down from the windowsill,

marched across the lobby and down the
stairs, not waiting for a ride in the elevator.
He went into the furnace room where it
was dark and gloomy and stayed there
three days.

The cooks tried to coax him out with tempting
scraps from the kitchen.

Miss Pritchett came down and brought him
a tuna sandwich.

Old Harry brought leftovers from the room
service trays.

"Come on," they all said, stroking his dusty
head. "It's not the same without you upstairs."

But Got To Go, who heard horrid little barking
noises up there, just turned his head away and
closed his eyes.

Then Mister Foster came down, kneeling on the dusty floor

in his good hotel manager pants and peering at Got To Go.

"My word," he said, "this won't do. The guests are asking for you. Where is Got To Go? they all say. We have to keep the guests happy, so come on, old boy, stop this nonsense and get upstairs where you belong." He stood up and swatted at his pants.

"Dust! Dirt! Cat hair! My word, doesn't anybody clean down here?" He sneezed a huge sneeze and took out his snowy white handkerchief. "And look at you, your coat's a mess. We can't have a hotel cat looking like that."

When Mister Foster left the furnace room Got To Go went with him. He was tired of it anyway.

And so Got To Go gradually got used to Arnie,

but life was not so good at the Sylvia Hotel.

It was not nearly as good.

For one thing, he hadn't brushed his whiskers for ages in Mister Foster's bathroom. And he had always had his afternoon nap on the windowsill in Mister Foster's office where it was quiet except for rain on the window sometimes and the scratching of Mister Foster's pen.

Now Arnie was in Mister Foster's office and Got To Go had to go downstairs for his afternoon nap, where there was no warm wide windowsill. Where there was no windowsill at all. Not even a window. Not even a sill. And no one making pen-scratching noises to put him to sleep.

yip!
yarp!
yip!

yarp!
yarp!

It seemed like Arnie never stopped barking

except when he slept or when Mister Foster
carried him around, which annoyed Got To
Go a lot. Worst of all, wherever Got To Go
went, Arnie ran circles around him,
barking hysterically. Got To Go, who was
much bigger than Arnie, just ignored
him, making him bark louder and run in
faster and faster circles.

yarp!
yarp!
yarp!

yip!
yip!

Then one day as Arnie dashed in front of him,

Got To Go leapt up in the air and came down smack on top of Arnie, flattening him onto the carpet in mid-bark. You could hardly see any of Arnie sticking out. It was very quiet in the Sylvia Hotel lobby.

Just as Mister Foster was thinking he should rescue Arnie, Got To Go got up, stepped over Arnie and carried on his way. Arnie, scared out of his wits, kept on barking and running in circles all by himself till Mister Foster picked him up and put him in his bed, where his feet kept running as he slept.

Arnie never chased Got To Go again.

Not even when Got To Go reclaimed his windowsill in Mister Foster's office for his afternoon naps, or jumped up on the sink to brush his whiskers against the toothbrush in Mister Foster's bathroom.

But Arnie still barked his irritating little bark

at everything and everyone else, annoying the guests and worrying Mister Foster. Arnie backed up with each bark like a little windup dog, sometimes tripping people who were not expecting a dog going the wrong way.

One morning Mister Foster had to go up on top of the Sylvia Hotel to talk to a man fixing the roof. He took Arnie with him.

Mister Foster set Arnie down on the roof. "Stay!" he said. Arnie stayed. (It was the only thing he had learned how to do.) Till a seagull flew past and he tore off after it, sailing right off the edge into the air and dropping out of sight.

When Mister Foster got down to the ground, Arnie was nowhere to be found.

"Arnie?" he called, clutching his chest and looking everywhere. "Arnie?"

Silence.

"Oh my word, oh my word, poor Arnie, he must be dead but where is he?" And he ran around in circles calling Arnie.

"Have you seen a small dog?" he asked some people walking past.

"No," said a man. "But I saw a leafy branch with some little feet under it going down the sidewalk and up the hotel steps."

In Mister Foster's office,

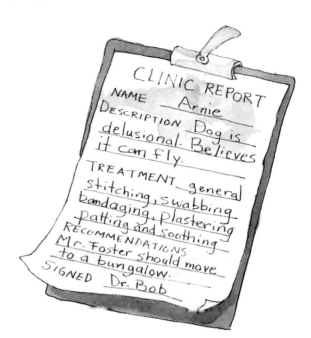

a quivering, leafy branch covered Arnie's bed.
Under it was Arnie. He had landed in the
big tree.

   Mister Foster drove Arnie to the dog doctor,
who laughed and said, "Well, Superdog, did you forget
your cape?"

   "Don't take any more animals up on eight-storey
buildings unless they have wings," he told Mister Foster.
"That will be forty dollars please."

   Mister Foster drove Arnie home in the rain.

   He had a headache. He had a lot of headaches lately.

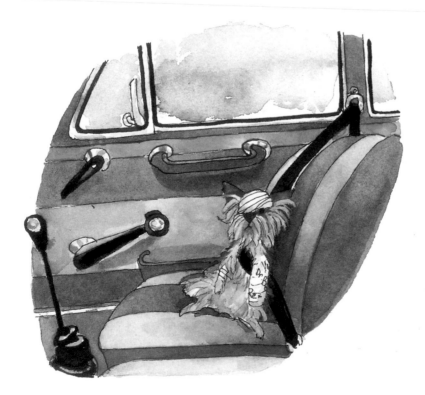

One fine day Old Harry, walking Arnie,

stopped to watch

the sailboats. A girl

came rollerblading by and Arnie

took off, yanking the leash from

Old Harry and knocking the girl off

the path into the bushes. And knocking

himself senseless, which was not hard to do.

When Old Harry told him what had happened,

Mister Foster got another headache.

Another day a man from the City Works

Department removed a sewer cap behind the hotel to fix a problem. Arnie darted outside and started barking at the man, backing up with every bark, and disappeared down the sewer. There was a moment's silence and then the hollow, far away sound of Arnie barking down there.

The man laughed and climbed down the ladder into the sewer. He came up holding a wet and dirty Arnie at arm's length.

"I think he needs a bath," the man said.

When Arnie was clean again, Mister Foster sat for a long time with his head in his hands, thinking. Then he made a long distance phone call. A very long distance phone call.

A week later, his friend Madame LaTour
from France arrived with a small dog that looked
a lot like Arnie. Her name was Fifi, and she was
very sweet. Her coat was a lovely shiny rust
colour and Madame LaTour brushed her every
morning and tied her hair up out of her bright
eyes with a ribbon, a different colour every day.

Arnie fell in love. He stopped barking
and spent all his time sitting outside Madame
LaTour's door, or in the room playing with Fifi
and taking French lessons.

When Madame LaTour said "Arrêt,
Arnie," Arnie stopped. When she said
"Ne bougez pas, Arnie," Arnie stayed.
And when she told him to stop barking,
Arnie stopped barking.

"Arnie is not naughty,"

Madame LaTour told Mister Foster,
"he is just nervous here. Too many people.
It is bad for Arnie."

And indeed it seemed as if it must be so.

"C'est beau! Fifi 'as fallen in love with
Arnie," Madame LaTour said. "I, too, 'ave
fallen in love with this dear little dog.
I would like to take him on a holiday."

"My word, what an interesting idea,"
said Mister Foster, smiling behind his
handkerchief. "I think this might be good
for Arnie."

Madame LaTour came with one dog.
She left with two.

And Got To Go smiled all over inside
himself as he watched them leave.

Mister Foster began receiving photographs in the mail

with Madame LaTour's handwriting underneath.

Finally, a letter came for Mister Foster. It was from Madame LaTour.

"Mon bon ami, I am writing to ask your kind permission to keep Arnie here with us. What can I say, mon ami? Fifi will be too sad without Arnie now. I think her little heart would break. Mine, too. Can he stay? S'il te plaît?"

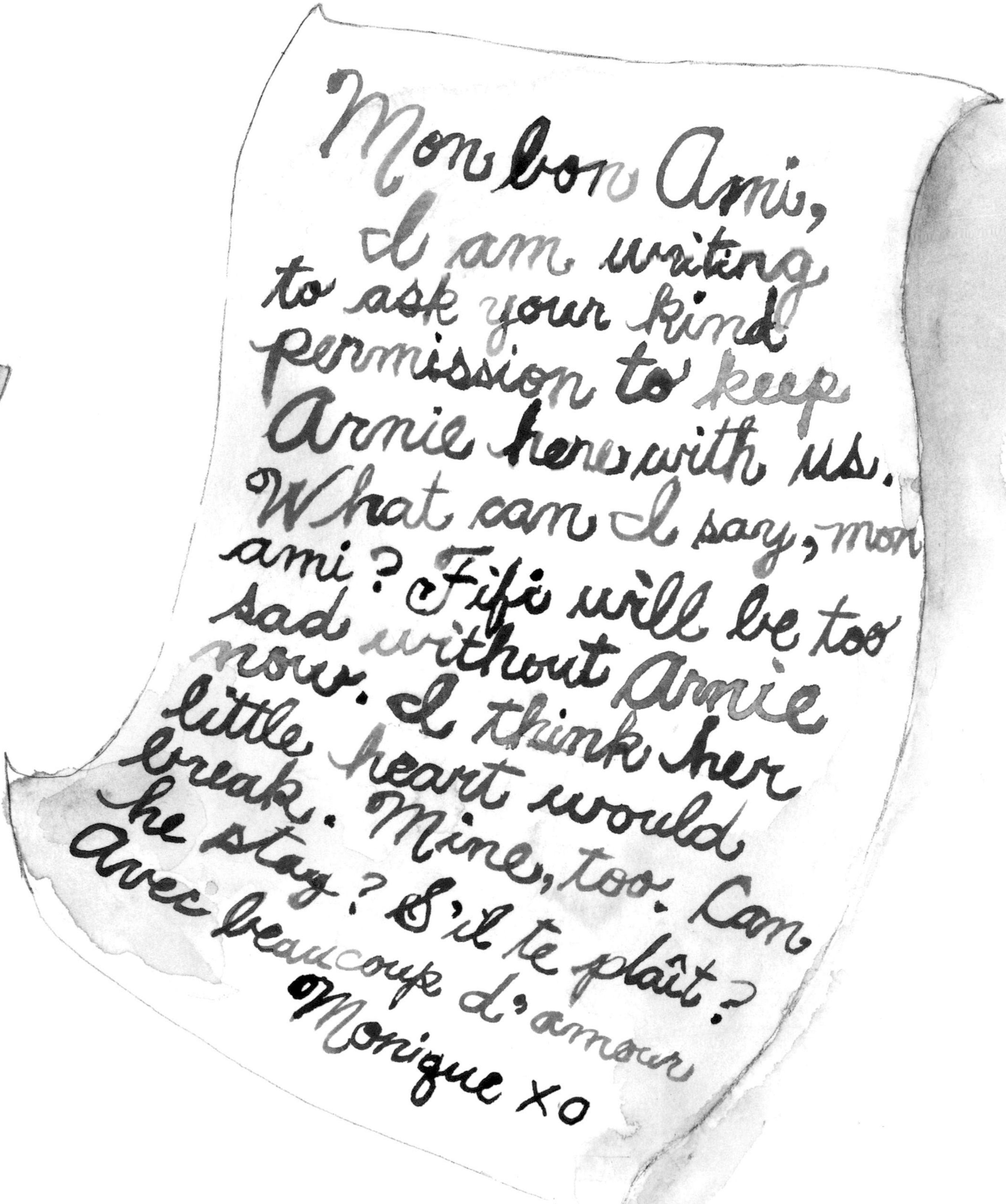

Mon bon Ami,
I am writing
to ask your kind
permission to keep
Arnie here with us.
What can I say, mon
ami? Fifi will be too
sad without Arnie
now. I think her
little heart would
break. Mine, too. Can
he stay? S'il te plaît?
Avec beaucoup d'amour,
Monique XO

Mister Foster shut the door of his office

and did a little dance.

"Oui!" he sang as he danced. "Oui oui oui oui!"

He sent a telegram.

He threw away his headache pills.

As he skipped out into the lobby he

saw Got To Go on the windowsill soaking up

the sun.

"My word," he said, "is that cat still here. As

soon as it stops raining that cat's got to go."

And Mister Foster buttoned his suit jacket and

hurried off to manage the hotel.

Got To Go, the sun warm

on his thick grey fur, closed his eyes and began to purr.

Life at the Sylvia Hotel was good. It was very, very good.

To Axel for the stories, and to Arnie for being Arnie.

—LS

For Zephyr. And for Paul, who invented the Mister Foster Dance.

—CN

Text copyright © 2001 by Lois Simmie

Artwork copyright © 2001 by Cynthia Nugent

Raincoast Books gratefully acknowledges the support of the Government of Canada through the Book Publishing
Industry Development Program, the Canada Council and the Department of Canadian Heritage. We also acknowledge
the assistance of the Province of British Columbia through the British Columbia Arts Council.

Jacket and interior design by Val Speidel
Printed and bound in Hong Kong, China
by Book Art Inc., Toronto

First published in 2001 by
Raincoast Books
9050 Shaughnessy Street
Vancouver, British Columbia
Canada, V6P 6E5
www.raincoast.com

In the United States:
Publlisher's group West
1700 Fourth Street
Berkeley, California
94710

10 9 8 7 6 5 4 3 2

NATIONAL LIBRARY OF CANADA CATALOGUING IN PUBLICATION DATA

Simmie, Lois, 1932–
Mister got to go and Arnie

ISBN 1-55192-494-3 (bound)   ISBN 1-55192-636-9 (pbk.)

I. Title.
PS8587.I314M57 2001   jC813'.54   C2001-910723-4
PR9199.3.S5185M57 2001

Yip yip!

Yarp!

Yarp!

Yarp